D0418256

For Rachel - IB

Oxford University Press, Great Clarendon Street, Oxford OX2 6DP

Oxford New York
Athens Auckland Bangkok Bogotá Buenos Aires
Calcutta Cape Town Chennai Dar es Salaam
Delhi Florence Hong Kong Istanbul Karachi
Kuala Lumpur Madrid Melbourne Mexico City
Mumbai Nairobi Paris São Paulo Singapore
Taipei Tokyo Toronto Warsaw

and associated companies in
Berlin Ibadan

Oxford is a trade mark of Oxford University Press

First published 1999

A CIP catalogue record for this book is available
from the British Library

ISBN 0 19 279032 3 (hardback)
ISBN 0 19 272364 2 (paperback)

Printed in Hong Kong

All By Myself

Ivan Bates

OXFORD
UNIVERSITY PRESS

EVERY MORNING, Maya and her mother had breakfast together. First they would nibble on some sweet, green grass. Then Maya's mother would reach her long trunk high into the branches of a tall tree and pick the juiciest leaves for them to eat together.

But one morning, Maya decided that things were going to be different. As usual, they had breakfast together, and as usual, they nibbled at the sweet, green grass.

But just as her mother was about to reach up and pick some juicy green leaves, Maya said, 'No! I want to do it.'

‘But you’re just a
little elephant,’ said
her mother.
‘I want to do it,’
said Maya,
‘all by myself.’
‘Very well,’ said
her mother.

Maya sat and looked at the tree. It was very tall. The leaves seemed very far away. And she was just a little elephant. She thought for a bit. 'I know what to do,' she said.

She searched around until she found a long, thin stick. She picked it up, marched over to the tree, and, stretching up as high as she could, swished at the branches above, to try and knock the leaves down.

But it was no good. The leaves didn’t fall.

A lazy old lion, who was snoozing nearby, came to see what all the swishing was for.

'If you like,' he yawned, 'I could climb up the tree and pick you some leaves. With my claws, you know, it's no trouble at all.'

'No, thank you,' said Maya politely. 'I want to do it, all by myself.'

Maya sat down and thought
a little harder.

Then she had another,
even better idea.

She ran down to
the muddy brown
water hole.

There she stretched out her trunk
and sucked up as much water as she
could (which was quite a lot for such
a little elephant).

When her trunk was full,
she bounced back to the
tall tree, paused, pointed
her trunk and blew!

WHOOOSH!

The water swooshed
into the tree, soaking
everyone around.
The branches splashed
and dripped . . .

. . . but it was no good,
the leaves didn't fall.

A bird who had been sunbathing at the top of the tree (and was now very wet) came down to see what all the splashing was about.

'What do you think you're doing?' she squawked, flapping the water off her wings.

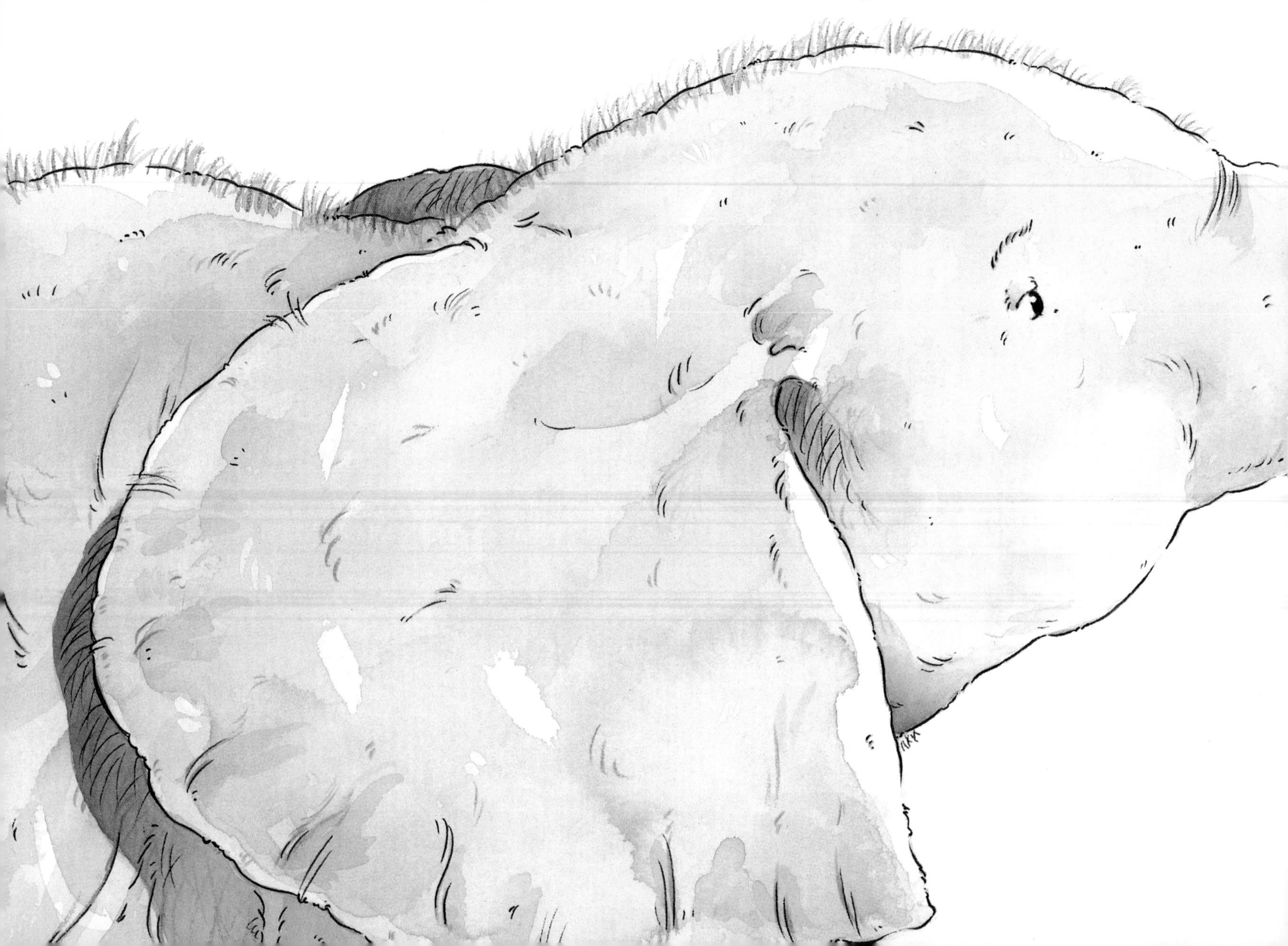

Maya explained it all very carefully.

'Is that it?' grumbled the bird. 'I will fly to the top of the tree and pick you some leaves. With my wings, you know, it's no trouble at all.'

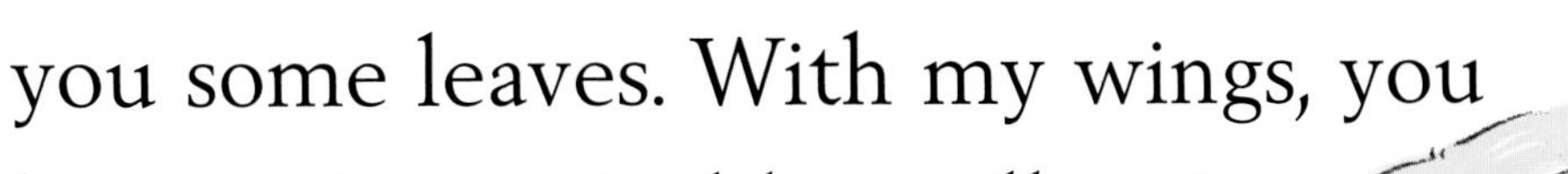

'No, thank you, ' said Maya. 'I want to do it, all by myself.'

'Please yourself,' said the bird.

Maya looked up at the tree and thought very hard indeed.

'I've got it,' she said finally.

Then she stepped back three paces, took a deep breath and charged at the tree, pushing it as hard as she could.

But it was no good. The tree didn't move and the leaves still didn't fall.

'My head hurts,' said Maya sadly.

Maya sat down at the bottom of the tall tree.

Suddenly a snake appeared from underneath a rock.

'If you like,' he hissed, 'I can slither up and pick you some juicy, green leaves. For me, you know, it's no trouble at all.' Maya shivered.

'No, thank you,'
she whispered.
'I want to do it,
all by myself.'

But this time Maya
had no ideas. It was
such a tall tree and
she was only a little
elephant. Then a voice
she knew very well
said gently,
'I have an idea.'

And with that, her mother carefully slipped her long tusks under Maya and, curling her trunk around, lifted her high into the branches of the tall tree. Maya stretched out her trunk and picked all the juiciest and greenest leaves she could.

She was a very happy little elephant.

Afterwards Maya and her mother looked at their delicious breakfast.
'You did it,' said her mother.
Maya thought for a moment.
'No,' she said slowly. '*We* did it. Together.'

And together they strolled
off across the plains as the
sun rose high in the sky.